# Great as a Button

Text by Masoud Malekyari © 2019 Magink Publishing House
Illustration by Sebastião Peixoto © 2019 Magink Publishing House
All rights reserved.
First Published in Germany by Magink Publishing House in Germany,
Kuglerstra Be 63, 10439 Berlin, Deutschland

Summary: It does not matter how small or ordinary you may look;
you are as important and great as you should be in this world and your
presence matters and is purposeful.

www.maginkbooks.com
info@maginkbooks.com
ISBN: 978-3-96656-002-3

# Great as a Button

Masoud Malekyari

Sebastião Peixoto

I am a black plastic button.

One day, I fell off a shirt in a fight between two kids. No one noticed. I thought to myself: "What good am I? I wish I were a pair of glasses, a house key, or even a sock so when I got lost, everyone would look for me." But I was just a black plastic button.

Every day, something new happened to me.
Some were
big...

and some were
small.

One day, I read a story about a king who wore beautiful clothes.
I said, "I wish I were a button on a king's coat so I could live
happily in a big castle."

But I was just a black plastic button.

I wanted to travel around the world...

But I was destined for something else.

Sometimes I got into trouble...

and sometimes I was very lucky...

Days passed and I was still at the tailor's shop, still asking myself:

## "what good am I?"

Botón Vermelho
Botón Carlantón
Botón Velichni
Marta Luz
Dolci d'Oro
Botón de Marinero
Brillantes

Every button was good for something...

But I was just a black plastic button.

Then one day the tailor gave me to a little boy
who put me in his pocket.

At first, I felt like I was in prison. Like heroes who are imprisoned.

I felt that soon enough I would become the leader of black plastic buttons in the big battle against the metal buttons.

I also thought all the other plastic buttons were waiting

for me to put them out of their misery.

But I was just a black plastic button…

Suddenly, that little boy took me
out of his pocket, and there was
light everywhere.

I felt cold on my back. I gently opened my eyes.

I felt like the whole world was watching me.

Had I become a button on a king's coat? Or the hero of all black

plastic buttons?

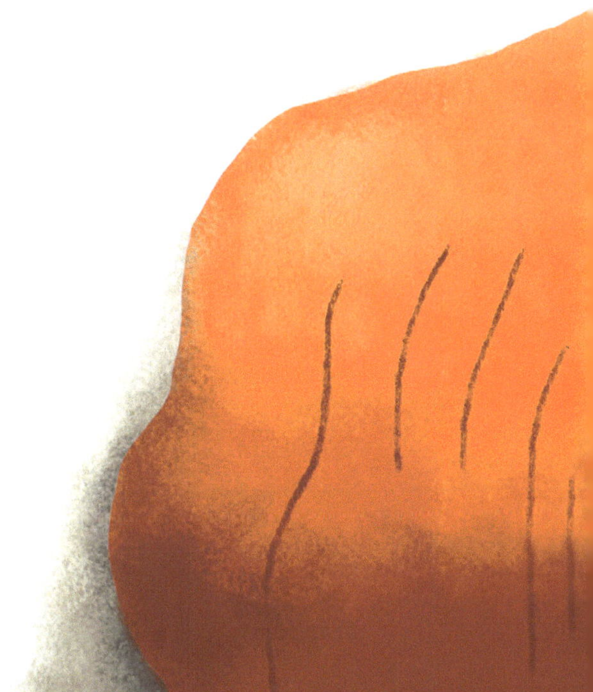

Neither!

I was still a black plastic button.

But I was

as great and important

as a button could be.

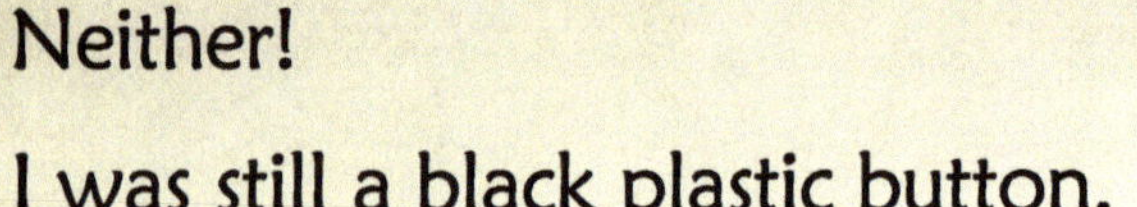